THE WORST BULLY IN THE ENTIRE UNIVERSE

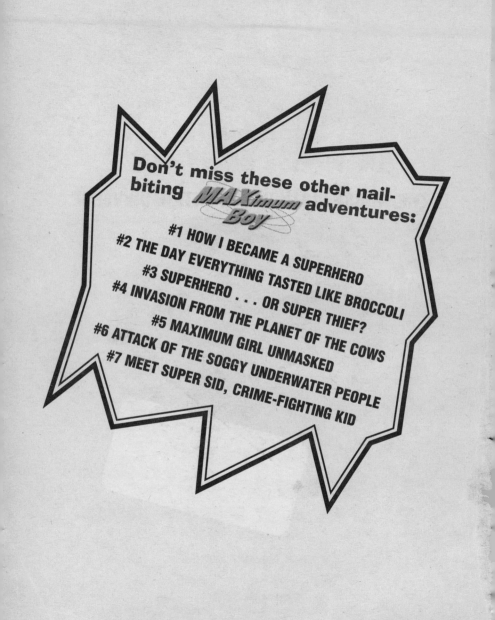

Don't miss these other nail-biting **MAXimum Boy** adventures:

MAXimum Boy

starring in

THE WORST BULLY IN THE ENTIRE UNIVERSE

BY DAN GREENBURG
ILLUSTRATIONS BY GREG SWEARINGEN

A Little Apple Paperback

SCHOLASTIC INC.
New York   Toronto   London   Auckland   Sydney
Mexico City   New Delhi   Hong Kong   Buenos Aires

ISBN 0-439-43939-6

Text copyright © 2003 by Dan Greenburg.
Illustrations copyright © 2003 by Scholastic Inc.

All rights reserved. Published by Scholastic Inc.

SCHOLASTIC, LITTLE APPLE, and associated logos are trademarks and/or registered trademarks of Scholastic Inc.

12 11 10 9 8 7 6 5 4 3 2 1   3 4 5 6 7 8/0

40

Printed in the U.S.A.
First printing, April 2003

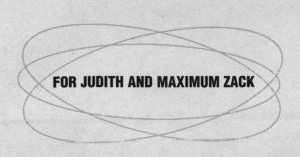

FOR JUDITH AND MAXIMUM ZACK

THE WORST BULLY IN THE ENTIRE UNIVERSE

CHAPTER 1

"Super Sid is a big fat liar," I said, hanging up the phone.

My mother, my father, and my annoying teenage sister, Tiffany, looked at me like I had just said the President of the United States was a chimpanzee. (Actually, at one time the President *was* a chimpanzee, but that's another story.)

"Max, what are you talking about?" asked

Tiffany. "Super Sid is a superhero. And about half an hour ago he helped save your life."

"I know that," I said. "But he also happens to be an impostor."

"How can you say that, Max?" said my mom. "Super Sid is such a polite boy. So well mannered. How could he be an impostor?"

"Politeness has nothing to do with impostorhood, Mom," I said. "Everything Super Sid told us about himself is a big fat lie. Like, he is *not* on the baseball, basketball, and football teams of the Thelma P. Flemm School in Cleveland. Like, he is *not* the president of his class. Like, he does *not* have a rock band called the Really Nice People. That was Tortoise Man on the phone just now. He found out the truth for me."

"Frankly, son, I think you're just jealous," said my dad.

"Braaaaaack!" said the blue-footed booby. It was the first thing I'd heard the bird say since Tiffany and Super Sid rescued it and me from the evil Dr. Zirkon.

OK, I think I might be going a little too fast for you here. Let me explain.

My name is Max Silver. I'm eleven and

I'm in the sixth grade. I live in Chicago with my parents and my annoying teenage sister, Tiffany. Three years ago, I was at the Air and Space Museum in Washington, D.C., where I accidentally handled some radioactive rocks that had just been brought back from outer space. All of a sudden I could do things most eleven-year-olds can't. Like fly. And lift eighteen-wheel trucks over my head with one hand. And run faster than the speed of sound. And say "rubber-baby-buggy-bumpers" really fast.

If I don't use my superpowers, I'm definitely the second-worst athlete in the sixth grade. But if I used them in school I'd blow my cover and put my family in danger. You might think I could use just a *little* of my superpowers and be just a *little* stronger and faster than other kids. Uh-uh. That's not how it works with superpowers. With super-powers it's all or nothing. I really hate that.

I do have a few weaknesses. I'm allergic to ragweed, milk, and math. Even *hearing* a math word problem makes me weak and nauseous. Superman had the exact same problem with kryptonite. I'm the only kid in the sixth grade with a doctor's note to get out of math class.

Because of my powers, the President of the United States is always sending me out on missions to battle the forces of evil. Like the time a mad scientist froze everybody on Earth for an hour and stole the world's greatest treasures. Or the time Iowa was invaded by evil cattle from the Planet of the Cows. Or the time Earth was invaded by soggy underwater people.

My teenage sister, Tiffany, got jealous of

all the attention I was getting. When her class took a trip to the Air and Space Museum, she broke into the space rocks exhibit and touched the same rocks that gave me my powers. OK, so it gave her superpowers, too, but she never really got the hang of how to use them.

Like, she never really learned how to fly. She's always bumping into birds and buildings and stuff. And she's not at all cool about having a secret identity. She keeps showing off and nearly blowing her cover. Also, she has a bad attitude about being a superhero.

OK, now this part is a little complicated, so pay attention. The last case the President asked us to solve involved a weird guy named Moth Man. Moth Man was eating holes in all the wool suits in Washington,

D.C. The President also assigned another superhero to the case, a guy who calls himself Super Sid. I hated Super Sid the minute I met him. He's four years older than me, and Tiffany wants to marry him. I'm not kidding you. I thought there was something phony about Super Sid, so I asked my buddy Tortoise Man to check him out.

Meanwhile, Tiffany and I set a trap for Moth Man, but while we're waiting for him on stakeout, she decides to go buy a fake fingernail to replace one she broke. A fake *fingernail*. Even though we're on a *stakeout*. I told you she had a bad attitude for a superhero. So while she's gone, Moth Man arrives. I overpower him. But then this creepy supervillain, Dr. Zirkon, shows up. He uses a math problem to knock me unconscious.

When I wake up, I'm in Zirkon's laboratory. I'm strapped to a table. On the next table is this huge bird from the Galápagos Islands, a blue-footed booby. Zirkon is just about to switch my brains with the booby's when Tiffany and Super Sid burst in and save us. Blah, blah, blah.

It's too late to take the booby back to the Galápagos tonight, so Tiffany and I bring him home to Chicago. Which is when Tortoise Man phones. He's done some checking and found out Super Sid is the phony I thought he was.

Now you know everything, so let's get back to where we left off.

"Well," said my mom, "whether Max is jealous or not, it's high time both you children are in bed. Tomorrow's a school day, you know."

"*Braaack,*" said the booby.

"Too bad we don't have anything to feed this bird," said Mom. "And it's too late to go out and buy birdseed."

"I don't think blue-footed boobies eat birdseed," I said.

The next morning, I got up early and dropped off the booby in the Galápagos Islands on the way to school.

The whole morning in school I couldn't stop thinking about Super Sid and what a big fat liar he was. I worried that the President might assign more cases to big fat liars. By lunchtime I couldn't stand it anymore. I decided to fly to Washington and warn the President. I went down to the boys' bathroom to change into my Maximum Boy uniform, but all the stalls were taken.

"Excuse me," I said. "How long are you going to be in there?"

"About five hours," said a voice.

"Well, I really need to get into a toilet," I said.

"You must be pretty tiny to fit into a toilet," said the voice. I heard laughter from the other stalls.

I thought I recognized the voice. It was Trevor Fartmeister, the school bully. Trevor Fartmeister is so scary that nobody even makes jokes about his name. He's a big heavy guy with a red buzz cut, and part of his ear is missing. They say that he lost part of his ear in a fight with a much bigger bully. They also say that Trevor bit off the other kid's nose.

With all the stalls occupied, I couldn't change into my Maximum Boy outfit. Do other superheroes have this problem, or was it just me? I could probably change into my outfit outside the stalls, but what if one of the boys came out of a stall while I was changing? Or what if somebody came in from the outside? It would blow my whole secret identity.

I walked upstairs and found a janitor's closet. Just as I was about to go inside and change, along came a teacher.

"Why are you going into the janitor's closet?" she asked.

"To get a . . . uh . . . monkey wrench," I said.

"What do you need with a monkey wrench?" she asked.

"I need it to . . . tighten my monkey," I said.

"Are you trying to be a smart aleck?" she said.

"No, ma'am," I said. "I'm sorry."

I went outside to the back of the school, crept behind a tree, and finally changed into my Maximum Boy uniform. Then I flew to Washington, D.C. When I landed on the White House lawn, the Marine guards recognized me.

The Marines escorted me into the White House. There in the Oval Office, sitting with the President, was Super Sid!

"Mr. President," I said, "I've come to warn you about Super Sid. He's an impostor and a big fat liar. Don't believe a word he says."

"What?" said the President.

"What are you talking about?" said Super Sid.

"I've done some investigating," I said.

"Super Sid is *not* on his high school baseball, basketball, or football teams. He is *not* the class president, and he does *not* have a rock band called the Really Nice People. What are you doing here, Super Sid?"

"Why, I'm warning the President about something important," said Super Sid. "I've just learned that a supervillain is planning to do something really embarrassing to the monument at Mount Rushmore. We need to go there and stop it before it happens."

"Mr. President," I said, "don't pay any attention to anything he says. He's a liar."

"I'm telling you the truth," said Super Sid. "You've got to believe me, not Max."

"Well, Super Sid," said the President. "I've known Max longer than I've known you. If I have to choose, I believe Max. So I won't take this Mount Rushmore business seriously. And now, if you boys will excuse me, I must get back to running the country and the free world."

We left the Oval Office. But outside, Super Sid was almost in tears.

"Max, I swear I'm not an impostor," he said. "Please check me out again. And please check out this Mount Rushmore business before it's too late. Please?"

I was starting to feel sorry for him. I sighed.

"OK, Super Sid. I'll check these things out for you," I said.

CHAPTER 2

I went to see Tortoise Man in his van under the bridge. Tortoise Man is a semi-retired superhero and a friend of mine. He's kind of old and kind of slow, but he's really, really nice.

"Super Sid swears he's not an impostor," I told Tortoise Man. "He begged me to check him out myself. Who told you he was an impostor?"

"A guy I know in Cleveland," said Tortoise Man. "His name is Paul Pimple-face."

"Well, in all fairness I think we ought to go to Cleveland and see this Paul Pimpleface in the flesh."

"Whatever you think," said Tortoise Man.

I scooped Tortoise Man up in my arms and leaped into the air. It normally takes me twenty minutes to fly from Washington, D.C. to Cleveland. With the added weight and wind resistance of Tortoise Man, it took me almost thirty.

Paul Pimpleface lived in a run-down part of Cleveland. We landed on a depressing-looking street and went from building to building, looking for his address.

Two tough guys saw us. They were both

about six feet tall and weighed maybe two hundred and fifty pounds each.

"Hey, looky here," said the first one. "It's an old geezer in a turtle suit and a dorky kid in a baseball uniform and cape. What do you think this is, Halloween?"

"Hey, bat boy!" said the second one. "Come here and give us some batting practice on your head." He held up an aluminum bat. They strolled over.

"Hey, Grandpa, why are you dressed like a turtle?" the first one asked.

"He's not your grandpa," I said. "And if you can't speak to him with respect, don't speak at all."

They burst out laughing. It was the funniest thing they'd heard all day.

"In case you're thinking of hitting me with that bat," I said, "I should warn you — I have fearsome powers."

They laughed so hard they almost peed in their pants. Then the one with the bat swung at my head.

I caught the bat in mid-swing and tied it into a knot. I clunked their heads together and dropped them on the ground.

"You're going to have nasty bumps on your heads now," I said. "Go home, apply ice, take two aspirins, and never pick on a skinny kid or an old man again."

We went off to find Paul Pimpleface. His apartment was in a basement hallway that stank of cat pee. We knocked on the door. A moment later we heard a voice on the other side of the door.

"What do you want?" it said.

"Are you Paul Pimpleface?" I asked.

"Who wants to know?" said the voice.

"Tortoise Man and Maximum Boy," I answered.

We heard several locks being unlocked, and then the door opened. Standing in the doorway was a ratlike little guy in a dirty robe and bunny slippers. He had yellow teeth and dirty fingernails. He needed a shave, a shower, and about a gallon of mouthwash.

He looked very familiar. And then I knew why.

"I know you," I said. "You're not Paul Pimpleface, you're Pete Delete."

Pete Delete was a nutty inventor and kind of a superhero groupie. He liked to hang out around the League of Superheroes and try to pretend he was one of them. With one of his inventions, I got him to erase the memories of kids at our school who figured out that my sister, Tiffany, was Maximum Girl. With another of his inventions he turned the President of the United States into a chimpanzee. I personally put him in jail for that one.

"How the heck did you get out of jail so soon?" I asked.

Pete Delete smiled slyly.

"Easy," he said. "I built another Mind-Eraser. I erased the minds of the guards and told them I was a visitor. Hey, you ain't gonna take me back to jail now, are you?"

"I might or I might not," I said. "I haven't decided yet."

"What do you want me to do?"

"You told Tortoise Man that Super Sid is an impostor," I said. "Super Sid swears he isn't. Is he or isn't he?'

"Super Sid is a big pain in the butt," said

Pete Delete. "He thinks he's such hot stuff. You ask me, he ain't worth a pitcher of warm spit."

"He may or may not be worth a pitcher of warm spit," I said. "But is he an impostor, or did he really do all the things he claims he did?"

"Oh, he probably did do all those things," said Pete Delete. "But he still ain't worth a pitcher of warm spit."

Oh, boy, did I ever feel stupid. I'd let my jealousy of Super Sid ruin my judgment. Worse yet, I let it get in the way of my job as a superhero. I had to do something right away with Super Sid's warning about trouble at Mount Rushmore.

"Tortoise Man," I said, "I think I'd better look into Mount Rushmore."

"Mount Rushmore?" said Pete Delete.

"They're talking about Mount Rushmore right now on the news."

"They are?" I said.

From inside Pete Delete's apartment I could hear the voice of a reporter talking excitedly on the TV. I pushed past Pete Delete into his apartment and got a nasty shock.

On the TV screen was a shot of Mount Rushmore, the national monument in the Black Hills of South Dakota that has huge stone sculptures of four U.S. presidents carved out of the mountainside — George Washington, Thomas Jefferson, Abraham Lincoln, and Theodore Roosevelt. Now attached to the faces of the presidents were . . . giant pairs of nose-glasses! Thick-rimmed glasses with huge fat noses and bushy moustaches attached to them.

CHAPTER 3

When I phoned the White House, they put me through to the President right away.

"Sir, I was way off base about Super Sid," I said. "I checked him out, and he isn't a big fat liar after all. But now we have this problem at Mount Rushmore. What do you want me to do about it?"

"Well," said the President, "we sure can't let those nose-glasses remain on the faces of the presidents. We'll be a laughingstock all over the world. Do you think you could get them down from there?"

"If somebody got those nose-glasses up there, sir," I said, "I can sure get them down."

"How long do you think it will take you?"

"That depends on whether Maximum Girl and Super Sid can help me. And on how much homework I have to do tonight."

"Now that I know Super Sid isn't a big fat liar," said the President, "I'd like to get him back to work on the hole in the ozone layer. Do you think you and Maximum Girl can do this together?"

"Sure," I said.

"Good," said the President. "Max, please get rid of those nose-glasses as soon as possible. It's a matter of national pride."

To get to Mount Rushmore I'd have to pass over Chicago, anyway, so I stopped off at home to get permission from my parents.

"Max, I thought you were in school," said my mom. "I had no idea you'd be flying all over Washington and Cleveland. And I don't much like this idea of you going to Mount Rushmore all of a sudden. What did you have for lunch?"

"Mom, I didn't have time to eat lunch yet," I said. "The President wants me to get rid of those nose-glasses as soon as possible. It's a matter of national pride."

"Well, Max, I'm sure the President doesn't want you to handle a matter of national pride on an empty stomach. How about a nice turkey sandwich with some lovely lettuce and tomatoes?"

"Fine," I said. "Is it OK if I take Tiffany out of school to help me?"

"Did Tiffany have her lunch?" she asked.

"How could I *possibly* know that? I haven't talked to her since breakfast."

"Please don't talk to me in a cranky voice, young man," said Mom. "You may be a superhero, but that doesn't mean you can speak to your mother in a cranky voice."

"I'm sorry if I sounded cranky, Mom," I said.

"Good. I'll make a nice turkey sandwich to take for Tiffany," she said.

I flew to school, changed out of my uniform, and went into Tiffany's history class. I told Tiffany's history teacher, Mrs. Hefty, that a family emergency had come up and

Tiffany had to go home. Then I went to Tiffany's desk.

"What are *you* doing here?" Tiffany asked. She didn't seem too glad to see me.

"Our, uh, friend in D.C. wants us to do him a favor," I said. "He wants us to do it as soon as possible. Mrs. Hefty says it's OK."

Tiffany rolled her eyes. "What kind of favor?" she asked.

I leaned close to Tiffany's ear and whispered right into it, "Somebody has put nose-glasses on all the presidential heads on Mount Rushmore. We have to get them off as soon as we can."

"Oh. If we left now, do you think we'd be back by three-thirty?" she asked.

"What happens at three-thirty?"

"I promised Heather and Ashley I'd go buy lipstick with them at the mall."

"We will definitely *not* be back by three-thirty," I said.

Tiffany let out this huge sigh. "I just don't see why I keep having to give up time with my friends to do these things," she said.

Tiffany has a really bad attitude about being a superhero. Did I mention that?

"Look, Tiffany," I whispered. "If you don't want to be a superhero anymore, just tell me. You can turn in your uniform and go back to being a normal teenage girl."

"Would I still have my superpowers?" she whispered.

"Sssshh!" I said. I looked around to see if anybody'd heard her. "I can't do anything about your powers," I said. "But if you use them for selfish things, the League of Superheroes will be all over you like fleas on a pup."

Tiffany let out another huge sigh. "Then let's just go and do it," she said.

"Mom sent you a turkey sandwich," I said. "You can eat it on the way."

"Goody, goody gumdrops," she said.

CHAPTER 4

To get to Mount Rushmore from Chicago, you fly over Illinois, Iowa, and most of South Dakota. Mount Rushmore is in the Black Hills, near the border of South Dakota. If you hit Wyoming, you've gone too far.

Tiffany was flying ahead of me, probably because she wanted to get this over with and be back in time to buy lipstick.

"Hey, Max, look over there!" she yelled. "There's Devil's Tower!"

"Devil's Tower is across the border in Wyoming! We've gone too far!"

"Ooh, I've always wanted to see Devil's Tower!" she yelled. "That was where the UFO came down in *Close Encounters of the Third Kind*. Can't we stop there?"

"I thought you were in a hot hurry to get home and buy lipstick!" I yelled. "The sooner we get rid of the nose-glasses on Mount Rushmore, the sooner you can go home and buy lipstick!"

"Fine!" she said in this really annoyed voice.

Tiffany made a sharp U-turn in the air and turned back toward South Dakota.

We were over Mount Rushmore in about three minutes. Even from the air we could see the nose-glasses. The four heads on Mount Rushmore had taken decades to carve out of the mountain. How could any-one put up nose-glasses so fast? And then I thought how — the person who had done this was a supervillain!

We landed on the top of Mount Rushmore and looked down at the nose-glasses. They were huge, and they seemed to be made out of some kind of gray plastic. I was glad to see that there were no TV news crews around. They must have just reported on the nose-glasses and left.

Tiffany and I carefully made our way down the face of George Washington and tried to see how the nose-glasses had been attached.

"It looks like the nose-glasses were stuck on with Krazy Glue," said Tiffany.

"I agree," I said. "Well, Krazy Glue is pretty hard to dissolve. But not if you have laser vision. Tiffany, do you know how to turn on your laser vision?"

"Well, *duh*," she said.

"Does duh mean yes?" I asked.

Tiffany rolled her eyes. She was wearing her mask, but I could tell.

"Yes, Max," she said. "I *do* know how to turn on my laser vision. Contrary to what you may think, I am not, like, an absolute *idiot*."

"Good," I said. "I'm glad you're not an absolute idiot."

Tiffany took the right side of Washington's nose, I took the left.

I turned on my own laser vision. I focused the red beam on the bridge of George Washington's nose and moved it around the outside of the nose-glasses. The laser made a nice sizzling sound as it worked. The nose-glasses came away from Washington's face.

All at once I heard a loud popping noise from the other side of the nose where Tiffany was working.

This was followed by a shower of sparks.

This was followed by a loud cracking noise.

This was followed by Tiffany saying, "Uh-oh."

Then, all at once, George Washington's nose cracked at the base and slid off his face. If I hadn't ducked at the last second, it would have taken me down with it.

I couldn't believe it. My stupid teenage sister had broken George Washington's nose right off his face! I stared at it with my mouth open as the nose bounced once on his chin and then started tumbling down the mountain.

"Tiffany! Look what you've done!" I shouted.

"I'm sorry, Max, OK?" she yelled. "I didn't do it on purpose!"

George Washington's nose went on tumbling down the mountain. I leaped into the air and dove down after it. I caught it just as it was about to smash on the rocks at the bottom of Mount Rushmore.

George Washington's nose was heavy. It weighed about as much as an SUV. I lifted it over my head with both hands and flew it back to the top of the mountain.

"The President is really going to be thrilled about *this*," I said.

"Do you have to tell him?" Tiffany asked.

"It'll probably make the six o'clock news tonight on every TV network plus CNN," I said. "I don't think I have to tell him."

"Well, I said I was sorry, Max. Like, what else do you want me to say?"

"I don't want you to say *anything*. I thought you knew how to use your laser vision. You said you knew how to use it."

"Well, I thought I did, OK? So I made a mistake. So big deal. I'm not a perfect person, OK? People make mistakes. Look, you've made mistakes, too."

"Maybe, but not like this. I never broke George Washington's nose off his face."

"Can't we, like, stick it back on with something?"

"With what, Krazy Glue? This nose is as heavy as a Jeep Cherokee. Krazy Glue would never hold it on there."

"Well, Max, you have powers I don't. Can't you melt rocks with X-ray vision or something?"

Hmmm. Tiffany was right. I *could* focus my X-ray vision and melt rocks. So maybe I could fit George Washington's nose back onto his face and make it stick.

"Tiffany, that's not such a bad idea. I'm going to give it a try."

"Cool."

I stood on George Washington's lower lip. I held his nose high over my head with both hands. I rested it against his face. Then I turned on my X-ray vision and focused it along the edges of the nose.

The rock where I was focusing my X-ray beam grew very hot. It glowed yellow, orange, then bright red. Molten rock, like lava, dripped down the bottom of the nose.

"Hey, look," said Tiffany. "Washington's nose is running."

"Funny," I said, grunting with the strain of holding the huge stone nose over my head and trying to melt it back into place.

After a while the nose seemed to be

sticking to Washington's face. I made my breath icy cold and focused it on the molten rock. The rock cooled fast. The nose stuck. If you hadn't seen it break off, you'd never know there was anything wrong with it. Except for the cooled lava that had collected at the bottom of Washington's nostrils.

"Eee-www, look," said Tiffany. "Boogers. Stone boogers."

It didn't take me and Tiffany long at all to laser the other three nose-glasses off Jefferson, Lincoln, and Roosevelt. Our national embarrassment was over.

The first thing I did when we got home was call Super Sid and apologize for calling him a big fat liar. He was a lot nicer about it than *I* would have been.

That night on the news they showed

the presidents' heads at Mount Rushmore.

"And so," said a newsman with a frowning face, "the huge nose-glasses that appeared so mysteriously on these gigantic presidential heads vanished as mysteriously as they had come."

"There's nothing *mysterious* about how the nose-glasses vanished, you jerk," said Tiffany to the TV screen. "*We* did it. Max, how come he didn't give us any credit?"

"Probably because he didn't know we did it," I said.

"Then why didn't we tell them?"

"Because that's not what superheroes do," I said. "Superheroes are modest. Superheroes care more about helping than about being praised."

"I think I might be a little more interested in being praised," said Tiffany.

"Well, at least you're honest about it," I said.

"Max! Tiffany!" Mom called. "Time to set the table!"

"And now," said the newsman, "we shall never know who or what caused these events to happen. Some say it's a mystery, like crop circles or Stonehenge. Some say it's the work of visitors from outer space. However, we may have a clue. A note was found at the top of Mount Rushmore. It reads as if it were left by whoever was responsible for the nose-glasses, and it seems to be written in rhyme."

"Children!" called Mom.

"Just a second, Mom!" I called back.

"Here, then," said the newsman, "is what the note said:

'I REALLY LIKED MY RUSHMORE PRANK.

IF YOU DID, TOO, IT'S ME YOU THANK.

TOMORROW I'LL BE IN L.A.

AT MALIBU I'LL SPOIL THEIR DAY.

SKIES WILL FILL WITH POOPING BIRDS,

AND CLOUDS WILL SPELL OUT NAUGHTY

WORDS.' "

"Tiffany, did you hear that?" I said. "The guy who did the nose-glasses at Mount Rushmore is now planning something tomorrow at Malibu Beach in Los Angeles."

"Of course I heard it," said Tiffany. "I'm not deaf, you know."

"Children!" Mom yelled. "If you don't come right now and set the table, you'll be grounded. There'll be no fighting for truth, justice, or the American way for an entire week!"

"We're coming, we're coming," I called.

We went into the kitchen, loaded up on plates, napkins, silverware, and glasses, and came back into the dining room.

"So do you think we should try and stop him?" I asked.

"Who are you trying to stop?" said Dad. He came in from the studio where he was working on an oil painting. My dad is a really great artist, but he gets paint all over the carpet and the walls.

"The guy who put the nose-glasses on Mount Rushmore is planning something else," I said. "Tomorrow, in Los Angeles."

"I see," said Dad. He took off his smock and got ready for dinner.

"What makes you think it's a guy?" said Tiffany. "Women do super-nasty things, too, Max."

"I know they do," I said. "Look, it doesn't matter if it's a man or a woman. The note said 'clouds will spell out naughty words.' What do you think that means?"

"Who knows?" said Tiffany. "Who cares? It's not our problem. Unless the President calls us and says it is."

Just then the phone rang. Mom answered it, then handed it to me.

"It's the President calling," she said.

CHAPTER 5

I took the phone.

"Max, I'm afraid we've got a problem in Los Angeles," said the President.

"You mean the clouds-spelling-out-naughty-words thing?"

"Yes," he said. "I don't know how this prankster plans to make clouds spell out naughty words, but we can't allow that sort of thing on our beaches."

"Why can't we?" I said.

"Max, would you want a small child in Los Angeles to look up in the sky tomorrow and see a cloud spelling out words like *wee-wee* or *poo-poo*?"

"Why not?" I said. "Little kids already know the words *wee-wee* and *poo-poo*."

"I just think it would have a bad effect on a child to look up in the sky and see clouds spelling out words like that. I want you to go to L.A. tomorrow and prevent it."

"Sir, I don't know where or when this thing is supposed to happen," I said. "How can I possibly prevent it?"

"You're the superhero, Max, not me," said the President. "I know you'll be able to figure it out." He hung up.

"The President wants me to go to L.A.

tomorrow and handle this clouds-spelling-out-naughty-words thing," I said.

"But, son, you're missing so much school lately," said Dad.

"I know," I said. "But how can I say no to the President of the United States?"

"I guess you're right," said Dad.

"So, Tiffany," I said, "you want to come with me?"

"Fat chance," Tiffany snorted.

And so the next morning, instead of going to school I flew alone to Malibu Beach. Don't get me wrong. I'm not complaining that I had to go to the beach instead of school. I just thought it was kind of a dumb mission.

I'd gotten up really early and I was tired. I flew up to thirty-thousand feet till I saw an airliner headed toward L.A. Then I grabbed onto its tail and let it tow me for a few hundred miles.

When I landed on Malibu Beach, I wasn't sorry I'd come. The sun was glinting off the water. The waves were crashing on the shore. It was beautiful. It was a school day, but there were lots of people on the beach. And lots of moms with little kids.

I had no idea when this thing with the clouds was going to happen, so I sat down to wait. I unsnapped my cape and spread it out on the sand. I lay down on it and looked up at the sky. The sky was a deep blue color. There wasn't a cloud anywhere in sight. I didn't see how anybody was going to be able to make naughty words out of the clouds if there were no clouds in sight.

By noon, nothing had happened, so I went and got a hot dog and a Dr. Pepper.

By three o'clock, still nothing had happened. I was beginning to think the whole thing was a hoax. Suddenly, I heard a small plane overhead. I looked upward. It was very high up, but I could tell by the sound it wasn't a jet. So it was weird that a jet trail started coming out of its tail.

No, it wasn't a jet trail, it was skywriting. Well, I've seen lots of skywriting planes at the beach. They advertise all kinds of things. Like this one now. Let's see, what was it advertising? T . . . U . . . S . . . Tuscan Yogurt, probably. I lay back on my cape and watched. And then, to my horror, I saw what the next letter was: T . . . U . . . S . . . H . . .

I shook out my cape and snapped it onto my uniform.

By now the skywriting had spelled out T . . . U . . . S . . . H . . . Y

Oh, no! A few of the little kids, those who were old enough to sound out words, were pointing upward and giggling. The President was going to really be upset.

I leaped into the air. I flew upward fast, till I reached the giant word TUSHY. I started fanning the air, breaking apart the letters.

The pilot of the skywriting plane called out to me:

"Hey, kid, leave those letters alone!"

I could see him in the cockpit of his little airplane. He was in a leather bomber jacket with a fur collar, a leather pilot's helmet, and goggles.

"Are you the guy who did the nose-glasses at Mount Rushmore?" I called.

"I don't do nose-glasses, I do skywriting!" he shouted. "For your information, I happen to be a great writer! Now will you please stop messing up my writing? You just ruined a perfect TUSHY!"

"Did somebody pay you to write TUSHY in the sky?" I yelled.

"Of course they paid me!" he shouted. "You think I'd be writing TUSHY in the sky for nothing?"

"Who paid you?" I yelled. "A kid or a grown-up?"

"I don't know!" he shouted. "I got a letter telling me what to do, with a lot of cash in it! Now get out of the way! I've got a lot more writing to do here!"

"What else did he pay you to write?" I yelled.

"None of your business!"

"It *is* my business!" I yelled. "The President of the United States has *made* it my business! What are you planning to write?"

"FART, if you must know!"

"I am not going to let you write FART in the sky!" I yelled.

"Why not? This is a free country, isn't it? You can't tell me what to write!"

"Yes, I can!" I yelled.

*　*　*

I was a failure at Malibu Beach. Lots of little kids saw TUSHY written all over the sky.

The newspaper headlines weren't kind, either:

PRANKSTER STRIKES AGAIN!

HUNDREDS WATCH BIG TUSHY IN SKY!

SKYWRITER SHOCKS BATHERS!

MAXIMUM BOY MESSES UP!

Mom and Dad tried to comfort me. They said it wasn't my fault. They said nobody else could have done any better.

The President called and said the same thing. I was pretty tired, so I went to bed early. Tomorrow was the day I'd been dreading all year.

CHAPTER 6

Today was the day I'd been dreading all year: P.E.E. Day. Physical Education Evaluation Day. On Phys. Ed. Evaluation Day, our gym teacher, Mrs. Hunkenhoffer, gives all the kids in every class a test to see how well they can perform certain stupid gym events. On Evaluation Day there are chin-ups, sit-ups, push-ups, rope climbing, and a whole lot more dumb activities like that.

Mrs. Hunkenhoffer is built like Arnold Schwarzenegger. She works out eighteen hours a day. I know that because she told us. Her arms are bigger than most people's thighs, but I could beat her up using my pinky finger on my left hand, and I'm a righty.

Before I got my superpowers, I used to hate Evaluation Day. I always did really lousy on almost every event, and the kids made fun of me. Now that I have my superpowers, I hate Evaluation Day even more. Because even though I can now do about a *thousand* more stupid chin-ups, push-ups and sit-ups than anybody in the school, I wouldn't. I can't afford to let anybody think I have superpowers because it would blow my stupid cover. And that really drives me crazy.

"Mom," I said, "I don't feel well this morning. Can I stay home from school? I've got a sore throat and a runny nose."

"Well, Max," she said, "just use your super-sore-throat-healer power and your super-runny-nose-drier power like you always do and you'll be fine."

See what I mean? Now I can't even stay home sick like normal kids.

"All right, class," called out Mrs. Hunkenhoffer. She held a clipboard and a stopwatch. There was a whistle around her neck. "Our first event is push-ups. Everybody down on the floor."

There were a few groans, but everybody got down on the floor.

"When I say, 'begin,' start doing as many push-ups as you can. I'd like each of

you to do at least twenty. All right . . . ready
. . . *begin!*"

Everybody started doing push-ups.
Before I got my superpowers I was able to do
only four. This time, although I could have
done push-ups all day long without even
getting winded, I stopped at five. I gave a
really big sigh and flopped on my belly.

"Five, Max?" said Mrs. Hunkenhoffer.
"Is that all you can do?"

"Yes, ma'am," I said. Boy, was this ever
humiliating!

"Why don't you at least try to do one
more?" she coaxed.

"I don't think I can, Mrs. Hunkenhoffer,"
I said. "I'm pooped. If I try to do one more, I'll
throw up."

"You know, Max," said Mrs. Hunkenhoffer, "I can do a hundred and fifty push-ups without breaking a sweat."

"Really? Well, I can hold up an eighteen-wheel tractor-trailer with one hand," I said. I don't know why I said that. It just slipped out. Everybody laughed.

"Please don't be sarcastic, Max," said Mrs. Hunkenhoffer.

Most of the other kids did at least ten push-ups, and quite a few did twenty. Trevor Fartmeister, the class bully, did forty-three. Whoop-dee-doodle-doo.

Trevor came over to me to brag. He always starts out by asking me how *I* did. Then he tells me how much better *he* did.

"How many push-ups did you do, Silver?" Trevor asked.

"Five," I said.

"*Five?*" he repeated, laughing. "*Girls* can do more than five push-ups, Silver. Tiny newborn *babies* can do more than five push-ups. *I* did—"

"Forty-three," I said. "I know. You're great, Trevor, you're really great. You're the best. You're *better* than the best. I wish I was you, Trevor, I mean it. My life has no meaning because I can't do forty-three push-ups, OK?"

Trevor looked at me strangely, then walked away shaking his head.

"The next event, class," said Mrs. Hunkenhoffer, "is the rope climb. I would like the first six students to take their places at the ropes."

Six thick ropes hung from the ceiling of the gym. Six kids went and took their places in front of each rope. I was not one of them. Trevor Fartmeister was.

"All right," said Mrs. Hunkenhoffer. "I want each of you to climb to the top as fast as you can, and then slide down to the bottom. On your marks . . . get set . . . *climb*!"

The six kids started up their ropes. Trevor Fartmeister was soon pulling ahead of everybody. I couldn't stand it. I focused my X-ray vision on his rope. I made it as hot as I could without having it burst into flames.

"Yowch!" said Trevor. He stopped and slid down the rope. He fell on the floor and stared at his hands.

"Why, Trevor, what's the matter?" said Mrs. Hunkenhoffer.

"That rope was *hot*," he said.

"That's called rope burn, Trevor. I'm

really surprised you didn't do better on the rope climb."

You know what? I really enjoyed that. In fact, I enjoyed it so much, I decided to do it some more. I began focusing on the other ropes. Wherever a kid was too good an athlete and too cocky about it, I made his rope hot. Wherever a kid was not a good athlete like me, I focused my X-ray vision on his muscles and gave him extra energy.

When we got to sit-ups, some kids got very mysterious stomachaches. Others didn't. And so on. By the end of Evaluation Day, Mrs. Hunkenhoffer was wearing a very confused expression on her face and shaking her head.

"Well, class," she said. "This has been a very surprising day. I'm very proud of some of our poorer athletes. And I'm very disappointed with some of our better ones. Yes, today has been a very surprising day."

If you want to know the truth, Evaluation Day is now my favorite day of the year.

CHAPTER 7

The President called us the next night during dinner.

"Hope I didn't interrupt your dinner," said the President.

"You did, sir, but that's OK," I said. "What's up?"

"Have you heard the prankster's latest note?"

"No, sir."

"OK, here it is. It says:

'I SEE LONDON, I SEE FRANCE,

I SEE EVERYONE'S UNDERPANTS.

GRANDMAS, UNCLES, KIDS, AND AUNTIES —

TOMORROW I'LL REVEAL THEIR PANTIES.' "

"Hmmm," I said.

"What do you think that means?" the President asked.

"I don't know, sir," I said. "It sounds as if somebody might try and pull down a lot of pants in London and France."

"That was our thinking, too," said the President. "Frankly, since the prankster seems to be American, we're afraid of getting the British and the French angry with us."

"But how can we stop somebody from

pulling down the pants of people in an entire city in England and in a whole country?"

"That's why I'm calling," said the President. "Any ideas?"

"Just a minute," I said. "Tiffany, Mom, Dad — the President says somebody's planning to pull down the pants of everyone in London and France. Is there anything we can do to stop them?"

"My heavens," said Mom. "Who'd ever want to do a fool thing like that?"

"Some really annoying kid," said Dad.

"Dad's got a point there," I said. "It does sound like some kind of kid. One with super-powers. But how would we stop him?"

"I suppose you could have people wear really tight belts," said Mom.

"You could suggest people hold onto their waistbands really firmly," said Dad.

"If the President thinks he's sending me to Europe to help people hang onto their pants, forget about it," said Tiffany.

"Sssshhh," I said, covering the mouth-piece. "You want him to hear you?"

"Well, is that how *you* want to spend the day tomorrow?" said Tiffany. "I personally have tests in math and social studies and a sleepover at Ashley's. And I'm not missing any of them to help people in Europe hold up their pants."

"Sir," I said into the telephone, "my family feels that there is nothing Tiffany or I can do to help."

"OK," said the President. "I'll get Super Sid to do it."

"Hang on a second, sir," I said. I put my hand over the phone. "Tiffany, if we don't handle this, the President is going to give it to Super Sid."

"Super Sid will get a lot of credit if he solves this, won't he?" said Tiffany.

"Yep."

"He'll be in all the newspapers and on TV," she said.

"Yep."

Tiffany sighed. "OK," she said. "Tell the President we'll do it."

CHAPTER 8

The President promised he'd call our teachers and get us excused from school. He also promised to make a few calls to London and Paris.

So, the next day we flew to London. As soon as we got there, Tiffany wanted to fly around and do some sight-seeing, but it was really foggy and we couldn't see much from the air. Well, we weren't here to see sights.

We were here to help the people of London keep their pants on.

We went straight to Number 10 Downing Street. That's where the Prime Minister lives. We knocked on his door. A cranky old man in a black uniform opened the door.

"Yes?" he said.

"Hi, there," I said. "I'm Maximum Boy and this is Maximum Girl. We're superheroes from America. We've come to see the Prime Minister."

"I'm afraid the Prime Minister can't see you today," said the old man. He made "can't" rhyme with "font."

"Why can't he see us?" asked Tiffany.

"The Prime Minister is having his tea," said the old man.

"Can we see him after his tea?" asked Tiffany.

"Quite impossible," said the old man. "After tea, the Prime Minister will be watching cricket on the telly. Come back tomorrow."

"By tomorrow it will be too late," said Tiffany. "Lots of people in London will have lost their pants. Including the Prime Minister. Including you."

"My word!" said the old man. "I shall tell the Prime Minister."

He left. A minute later another man appeared. He looked much younger than the one who opened the door. He was sipping tea from a cup.

"Hi," I said. "I'm Maximum Boy and this is Maximum Girl. We're superheroes from America."

"Smashing," said the younger man. "I'm

the Prime Minister. What's all this about me losing my pants?"

"Sir," said Tiffany, "some jerk is doing pranks — maybe you've heard about him? He put giant nose-glasses on the heads at Mount Rushmore. He got a skywriter to write the word TUSHY in the sky above Malibu Beach. He —"

"Ah, yes, quite," said the Prime Minister. "I've heard about the tushy thing."

"Anyway," I said, "tomorrow he's threatening to pull down a lot of pants in London. The President of the United States has sent us here to help you."

"Smashing!" said the Prime Minister. "You Yanks have always helped us in times of trouble. You came to our aid in World War Two. And now you've sent us superheroes to

save us from a chap who wants to pull down our pants. What do you suggest we do?"

"Well," said Tiffany, "maybe you could go on TV and tell people to make their belts extra tight tomorrow. Maybe also tell them to wear suspenders."

"Hmmm," said the Prime Minister. "And what will you two superheroes do?"

"Well," I said, "we could help people hold up their pants."

"How many pairs of pants do you think you could help hold up?"

"Uh, well, I could stand between two of them and hold up their pants," I said. "And Tiffany could stand between two more of them . . ."

"So . . . four?" said the Prime Minister.

"Uh, yeah," I said. "Four is about all we could probably manage."

The Prime Minister seemed disappointed.

"Well," he said, "if you help us all day long, at least you'll save four of our citizens from the embarrassment of losing their pants."

"Oh, we can't stay with you all day tomorrow," said Tiffany. "In the afternoon we have to go save France."

We flew to Paris to meet with the President of France.

He was very polite, but I don't think he knew who we were. Also, it didn't seem like he'd heard about the prankster.

"He put giant nose-glasses on the faces at Mount Rushmore," I said. "Did you hear about that?"

The French President frowned and shook his head.

"What ees thees nose-glasses you speak of?" he asked.

"They're glasses with big plastic noses and mustaches attached," said Tiffany.

The French President frowned and shook his head.

"The prankster also hired a skywriting plane to write the word TUSHY in the sky above Malibu Beach," I said.

The French President raised his eyebrows and nodded.

"Ah, ze beeg tooshee een ze sky!" he said happily. "Of *course* we have heard of ze beeg tooshee een ze sky! Everybody een *France* has heard of ze beeg tooshee een ze sky!"

We told the French President about the

prankster's plan to pull down the pants of everybody in France. And when we explained what we were going to do to help, he had about the same reaction as the Prime Minister of England.

Anyway, we spent the morning in London and the afternoon in Paris. In both places, somebody, moving faster than the eye could see, whizzed through town. He swiped thousands of belts and suspenders. He left thousands of English and French people with their pants down around their ankles.

Lots of people, like the Queen of England, were wearing underpants. There were embarrassing pictures in the newspapers and on TV.

The President of the United States had been worried that people in both England

and France would be mad at America for what happened. He was right.

YANK PRANKSTER YANKS BRIT PANTS! screamed the headlines in London newspapers.

FRANCE PANTS PULLED DOWN BY ZE AMERICAN WHO MAKE ZE BEEG TOOSHEE EEN ZE SKY! screamed the headlines in Paris newspapers.

Tiffany and I flew home. We felt bad that we couldn't do anything to help. Mom and Dad tried to make us feel better. It didn't help. We'd been beaten.

Whoever did this had moved too fast for a normal human. Only somebody with superpowers could have moved that fast. Somebody young enough to pull gross pranks. We couldn't think of anyone it could be.

Superboy? No, no way Superboy could have done this. Captain Marvel Junior? Not in a million years could Captain Marvel Junior have pulled off that many pants. No, it had to be somebody completely new to the business. Someone we'd never heard of.

The President phoned us.

"Did I say that this would happen or didn't I?" asked the President.

"Yes, sir, you did," I said.

"There's no proof the prankster is an American," he said. "Just because the first two pranks were in the United States is no proof he's an American."

"True," I said.

"Well, at least we tried," said the President. "At least you guys went over there to London and Paris and tried to help."

"Right," I said. I felt really awful.

CHAPTER 9

We didn't hear anything more from the prankster for about a week. And then one night the President phoned again.

"Max," said the President, "we have a new threat. Have you heard the prankster's latest note?"

"No, sir, I haven't," I said.

"Here it is," said the President:

" 'MILLIONS SIT

ON A WHITE COMMODE,

SURE THAT IT WILL

NOT EXPLODE.

BUT HIGH-PITCHED SOUNDS

WILL SHATTER GLASS,

AND PORCELAIN,

AND FROZEN GRASS.' "

"What does *commode* mean?" I asked.

"Toilet," said the President.

"Hmmm," I said. "Well, most toilets are made of porcelain . . ."

"And?" said the President.

"And, like he says, certain high-pitched sounds will shatter glass," I said. "Maybe others will shatter porcelain. It could be that this guy plans to find a frequency of sound that will shatter toilets. Maybe all the toilets in the country. Or in the world."

"And what's this about frozen grass?" asked the President.

"I don't know," I said. "Maybe he just couldn't come up with a good rhyme for glass."

"That's what *we* thought, too," said the President. "Now, I checked this out with our sound technicians. They know the frequency at which sound can shatter porcelain. But the only way he could produce a sound loud enough to shatter toilets all over the country is to bounce it off a satellite dish in outer space. Our sound guys figured out exactly where he'd have to put a dish to do that. We were hoping you and your sister might be willing to go out into space and intercept him when he tries it."

"Let me see if I'm getting this right, sir," I said. "You want me and Tiffany to fly into outer space and wait for this guy to appear on a space satellite dish?"

"I think you'd have a great chance of catching him."

"Sir, don't you think such a mission would be . . . kind of dangerous?"

"Very dangerous, Max. But I am willing to let you do it, anyway. The thought of every toilet in the country exploding . . . The thought of all that sewage . . . Well, that's what finally made up my mind."

"I see," I said. "Well, sir, I'll have to ask my family."

"Absolutely."

I turned away from the phone.

"Mom, Dad, Tiffany," I said. "The President of the United States wants to send me and Tiffany out on a dangerous mission."

"Oh, great," said Tiffany. "Just when I was planning to reorganize all my makeup."

"The President thinks the prankster is going to take a satellite dish up into outer space. A dish that can carry a sound that will explode toilets all over the country. He'd like us to go into space and intercept this guy."

"Max," said Mom, "that sounds too dangerous."

"Yes," said Dad, "far too dangerous."

"The President *knows* it's dangerous," I said. "But he's willing to let us do it anyway."

"Is there any air in space?" asked my Dad.

"No," I said. "But I've been there before and that didn't seem to be a problem."

"Max, isn't it very cold in space?" asked my mom.

"It's minus 270 degrees Celsius. That's minus 454 degrees Fahrenheit," I said.

"Well, you'd have to take your warm sweater, your mittens, *and* your earmuffs," said my mom.

CHAPTER 10

Sometimes, I don't listen to my mom. This time I did, and was I ever glad. Even with our sweaters, earmuffs, and mittens, Tiffany and I were plenty cold, flying upward through space.

When you're in space, everything looks black. There are tiny pinpoints of light, each of which is a star the size of our sun or bigger. Here's what really kills me: The light traveling from each star takes millions of years to get here. Don't ask me why. Maybe the light stops at lots of fast-food places on the way for Happy Meals and burritos. I mean it's traveling at the speed of light, which is a hundred and eighty-six thousand miles per second, and it *still* takes millions of years to get here.

I have to tell you what Earth looks like when you're up in space. It looks like one of those spinning globes they have in your school library, only there are swirls of white all over it. The white is cloud banks. You look down on Earth, and you can't see much besides the oceans, the cloud banks, and maybe a few tan smudges for continents. You can't see your unfinished homework. You can't see the school bully. You can't see anything much smaller than China. It kind of makes you think.

"Great view, huh, Tiff?" I said.

"Yeah," she said. "But my hair spray froze on my hair. If anything hits it, I'm going to have shattered hair. I can hardly wait."

Way up above us was the moon. It was full.

Just above us, and a little to the right, was the satellite dish the President told us to look out for. And it was just about where he said it would be.

"Hey, you dorks!" yelled a voice overhead.

I looked up. Standing on the satellite dish was a kid. A very large kid. He wore a black mask, a green sweatshirt, black shorts, and black high-top sneakers. On his shirt were white letters that spelled out NASTYBOY.

"What are you doing way up here?" shouted Nastyboy.

"So it's *you* who's been doing all these pranks?" I yelled back.

"Right, booger-nose!" he shouted.

"Watch out who you call names!" I yelled.

"What did you say, butt-cheek face?" called Nastyboy.

"I said watch out who you call names!" I yelled.

"Why should I do that, fart-blossom?" called Nastyboy.

"Because I said so!" I yelled.

"I thought you were a smart feller,"

called Nastyboy. "But I was wrong, you're a fart smeller!"

"Sticks and stones may break my bones, but names will never hurt me!" I yelled.

"Well, I don't care about *hurting* you if I can break your *bones*!" called Nastyboy.

He reached into a back pocket, took out some sticks and stones, and threw them at me. Luckily, my superpowers protected me. The sticks and stones didn't even hurt. They just bounced off me into infinite space.

"Sticks and stones don't hurt me, either, stinky-toes!" I yelled.

"I'm rubber, you're glue — whatever you say bounces off of me and sticks to you!" screamed Nastyboy. He took out a water pistol and squirted me with glowing green liquid.

"Sweat sock-mouth!" I yelled.

Amazingly, my words formed big, glowing green letters as they left my mouth. The letters spelled out SWEAT SOCK-MOUTH, and they hit Nastyboy. Then they bounced off of Nastyboy, came back, and stuck to my chest. It must have had something to do with that glowing green liquid.

"What did you call me?" shouted Nastyboy.

"Underpants-breath!" yelled Tiffany.

Her words formed big, glowing green letters as they left her mouth: UNDERPANTS-BREATH. The letters bounced off Nastyboy, came back, and stuck to Tiffany's uniform.

"I didn't hear that!" shouted Nastyboy. "What did you call me?"

"Porta Potti-breath!" I yelled.

Glowing green letters spelling PORTA POTTI-BREATH flew out of my mouth, bounced off Nastyboy, and stuck to my uniform. This was really weird. I had never seen anything like this before. This Nastyboy had some strange powers.

I flew up to the top of the satellite dish to get a better look at him. So did Tiffany. The letters peeled off us and floated lazily off into space.

Nastyboy was tall and fat and had a red buzz cut. He looked kind of familiar, but I couldn't remember if I'd ever seen him before.

"Who the heck are you?" I said.

"What's the matter, four-eyes, can't you read?" said Nastyboy. He pointed to the word NASTYBOY on his chest.

"Are you the guy who's been pulling all

these pranks?" asked Tiffany. "The nose-glasses on Mount Rushmore and all the rest?"

"Yeah," said Nastyboy. "What of it?"

"Why'd you do it?" asked Tiffany.

"For a laugh — what else?" said Nastyboy.

"Well, it's not funny," I said.

"That's what *you* think, smelly-pants," said Nastyboy.

I couldn't figure out where I'd seen him before. And then I knew. I had seen him in school. Nastyboy was our school bully, Trevor Fartmeister — but now he had super-powers!

CHAPTER 11

Trevor Fartmeister is always picking on smaller kids in school, like me. He trips them, he makes fun of them, he takes their lunch money, he gives them wedgies, he throws them in trash cans.

The fact that the biggest bully in our school now had superpowers meant that he was about a thousand times more dangerous than before. It also meant that he was now the biggest bully in the whole entire universe. We had to somehow neutralize his powers. But right now we had to disarm the satellite, or else every toilet in the country was about to explode.

"I know who you are," I said. "You're Trevor Fartmeister."

Nastyboy looked like I had punched him in the stomach.

"What?" he said. "Where did you get that name?"

"It's a stinky name and it's stinking up all of outer space," said Tiffany. "They can probably smell your name on the moon."

Suddenly, Nastyboy went berserk. Screaming like a banshee, he flew at Tiffany in a rage. She punched him in the belly, and sent him about fifty yards into space. There's no gravity in space, by the way. So that might explain how far he flew from just one punch.

I smashed my fist through the middle of the satellite dish. It came out the other side and left a big hole.

Nastyboy bounced back. "What have you done to my satellite?" he screamed.

"I ruined it," I said. "I made it impossible for you to send the beam to Earth that will shatter porcelain."

"You haven't ruined that satellite!" he said. "It'll still send the beam unless I personally disarm it. And I sure ain't about to do *that!*"

He flew at me with all his might. I was waiting for him. I had it timed perfectly. I drop-kicked him so hard, he went hurtling off into space. Tiffany and I watched him go.

Pretty soon he was only a dot in the distance. Then he completely disappeared.

Since neither of us knew how to disarm the satellite, there was nothing else to do for now but go home. Tiffany and I flew back to Earth.

CHAPTER 12

Tiffany and I decided on a bold move. We went to see Nastyboy's parents. They lived on the third floor of an apartment building on the north side of Chicago.

Mr. and Mrs. Waldo Fartmeister weren't monsters. In fact, they were sort of nice.

"So you're the famous Maximum Boy and Maximum Girl," said Mrs. Fartmeister.

"We've heard so much about you. You must be very brave."

"You say you know our son, Trevor?" asked Mr. Fartmeister.

"Only professionally," I said. "Are you aware that he calls himself Nastyboy?"

Mr. and Mrs. Fartmeister looked at each other and sighed.

"We know," said Mrs. Fartmeister.

"Where did he get those strange powers of his?" asked Tiffany.

"At Dr. Shmendrick's office," said Mrs. Fartmeister.

"Excuse me?" said Tiffany.

"We brought him to Dr. Shmendrick to have his annual school checkup," said Mr. Fartmeister. "It was a very stormy day. Heavy rain, thunder, lots of lightning flashes. Anyway, it was while he was in the X-ray machine that it happened."

"What happened?" I said.

"Lightning struck the machine," said Mr. Fartmeister. "It came in through an open window and hit it. There was a terrible flash. Poor Trevor screamed. I thought for sure it had fried him up like a hamburger patty. But by some miracle, he was all right."

"That's when the strange behavior started," said Mrs. Fartmeister. "We're simple people. We find it embarrassing."

"Like what kind of behavior are you talking about?" Tiffany asked.

"Like glowing in the dark, for one thing," said Mr. Fartmeister.

"Glowing in the dark is nothing," I said. "Both Maximum Girl and I do that."

"Is that a fact?" said Mrs. Fartmeister.

"How about that! Waldo, did you hear what the young man said? He and the girl glow, too."

That seemed to make her happy, knowing other kids glowed in the dark.

"What behavior besides glowing in the dark?" asked Tiffany.

"Well, you know," said Mr. Fartmeister. "The tremendous strength. The bouncing. I mean, Trevor is a big boy. A *big* boy. He was always strong. But he'd never picked up a bus before. When we left the doctor's office and went outside, though, darned if he didn't pick up a Michigan Avenue bus. 'Hey, Dad,' he said. 'Look at me. I picked up a Michigan Avenue bus.' Of course, the bus driver and the passengers weren't too pleased with Trevor. I made him put it down."

"You mentioned bouncing," I said.

"That's how Trevor gets around," said Mrs. Fartmeister. "He bounces. After he put down the bus, he grabbed us in both arms and bounced us home. I must say, it beats the subway. Say, would you kids like some milk and cookies?"

"No, thanks," I said. "You folks seem to just be impressed by what your son is doing. But he's actually causing a great deal of trouble. People could get hurt."

Mr. and Mrs. Fartmeister looked at each other and sighed.

"What can *we* do?" said Mr. Fartmeister. "We're only his parents."

"Well, there's a lot you could do," I said. "Like you could forbid him to do these things. That's what parents are supposed to do, isn't it?"

"Oh, he'd never listen to *us*," said Mrs. Fartmeister.

"Then maybe you could, like, punish him?" said Tiffany.

"We couldn't punish him," said Mr. Fartmeister. "He's our little boy."

"Why not just ground him? Take away some of his privileges?"

"Oh, we couldn't take away any of his privileges," said Mrs. Fartmeister. "We wouldn't want him to be mad at us."

"If *you* don't stop him," I said, "then *we'll* have to. And you may not like the way we do it."

"Just so long as you don't hurt him. He's such a delicate thing," said his mother.

CHAPTER 13

In Cleveland, Pete Delete was still in his filthy robe and bunny slippers. And he still smelled like he hadn't taken a shower.

"OK, Pete," I said. "Here's your big chance to do me a favor."

"Refresh my memory," said Pete Delete. "Why am I doing you this favor?"

"Because we're not taking you back to prison where you belong," said Tiffany.

"Oh, right, now I remember," said Pete Delete.

"Now, I know you're a pretty good inventor, Pete," I said. "And I may need to use that Mind-Eraser of yours in a little while. But here's what I want to know now. In all your years of hanging around the League of Superheroes as a groupie, did you ever invent a machine that could dissolve superpowers?"

Pete Delete flashed me a fishy smile.

"You mean like math word problems dissolve *yours*?"

Uh-oh. I didn't realize Pete knew my one weakness. What if he suddenly pulled a math problem on me? What power would Maximum Boy have over him then?

And then I remembered Tiffany. Whatever weaknesses she had, losing her powers over math problems wasn't one of them. If

Pete Delete temporarily took away *my* powers, Tiffany would punch him out like she did Nastyboy in outer space.

"Yeah," I said. "Something like that. What have you got?"

Pete Delete chuckled, scratched himself, and belched.

"Well," he said. "Years ago I invented a little gizmo you might like. I call it the Power Blacker-Outer. You turn it on, press it against a superhero and — whammo!"

"Whammo?" I said.

"The Power Blacker-Outer figures out the superhero's powers," he said. "Then it shuts those powers right down."

"Permanently?" said Tiffany.

"Nah, temporarily," said Pete Delete. "But you can set the dial for however long you want the powers shut down."

"And this thing really works, huh?" I asked.

"Who knows?" said Pete Delete. "I've never tried it."

OK. Not exactly the answer I was looking for, but I didn't have much choice. Tiffany and I had to locate Nastyboy, press the Power Blacker-Outer against him, and pray that it worked. I didn't know where to look for Nastyboy. I *did* know where to look for Trevor Fartmeister.

We took along the Power Blacker-Outer. Just to be on the safe side, we also took along the Mind-Eraser. And its inventor.

Tiffany, Pete Delete, and I caught up with Trevor Fartmeister at a little after three P.M. as he was leaving school. Tiffany and I were still in our superhero uniforms.

"Well, well, well. Look who's here," I said. "Trevor Fartmeister, the nastiest boy in the entire universe."

Trevor looked startled. "What are you doing here?" he said.

"We've come with a message from the League of Superheroes," said Tiffany.

I looked at Tiffany and frowned. Besides me, she has never even *met* a member of the League of Superheroes.

"What's the message?" asked Trevor.

Tiffany took a piece of paper out of her pocket and started reading:

" 'Dear Nastyboy: Unless you go up in space and disarm that satellite by sunset today, we are going to use your body as a dummy for martial arts training. Check in with Maximum Boy and Maximum Girl at seven-thirty, right outside the school yard,

when you get back. Yours very truly, The League of Superheroes.' "

"Maybe they're just kidding around," he said.

Tiffany and I both laughed. So did Pete Delete.

"The League of Superheroes *never* kids around, fat boy," said Pete Delete. "You know, you *would* make a great martial arts dummy. I wouldn't mind giving you a couple of karate chops myself."

"What time is sunset today?" asked Trevor.

"Seven-twenty-three," I said. "That gives you just about four hours."

"Where do they want me to meet you when I get back?" he asked.

"Right here," I said. "Right outside the school yard. At seven-thirty."

Trevor nodded again. Then he tore off his shirt, revealing his Nastyboy uniform. He pulled a Nastyboy mask out of his pocket. He took a long running start, did two practice bounces, and then soared into the sky and disappeared.

CHAPTER 14

"You have to go *where* at seven-thirty?" asked my mom.

"Nastyboy is coming back from outer space, right after he disarms the space satellite that blows up toilets," I said. "He has to meet us at the school yard, so the League of Superheroes doesn't use him for target practice. So is it OK if we go to the school yard?"

"Just be sure the dishes are washed and

dried and put away in the cupboard above the sink," she said. She frowned at Pete Delete in his filthy bathrobe and bunny slippers. "Would your friend like to stay for dinner?"

"I'd be *honored* to stay for dinner, ma'am," said Pete Delete.

"Well, you can get cleaned up in the bathroom at the end of the hall," she said. "There are bath towels in there and an electric razor. I suggest you use them. And, Max, you can lend your friend some fresh clothes from Dad's closet."

When Pete Delete came out of the bathroom, we almost didn't recognize him. He was wearing a clean pair of jeans and a checkered shirt. The filthy robe and bunny slippers were nowhere in sight. He looked and smelled clean, and he had even shaved. Mom was impressed.

"So what type of business are you in, Mr. Delete?" said Dad at dinner.

"I'm an inventor," said Pete Delete.

"Really?" said Dad. "Would I have heard of any of your inventions?"

"Remember when the President of the United States got turned into a chimp?" said Pete Delete. "I was the guy who turned him back into a person again."

"Well done," said Dad.

Pete forgot to mention that he was also the guy who'd turned the President into a chimp to begin with, but that's another story.

Right after dinner, Tiffany, Pete, and I did the dishes. Then we went to the school yard to see if Trevor Fartmeister had come back from outer space.

There was nobody at the school yard

when we arrived. I looked at my watch. It was 7:30. The sun had just set.

7:45, and no Trevor.

8:00 and still no Trevor. Had he changed his mind about disarming the satellite? Had he figured out Tiffany was bluffing? What would we do if he was on to us?

At 8:13, we saw something. A tiny speck in the sky, growing larger. A moment later, Nastyboy landed heavily in front of us. He was covered with dirt and ash and he seemed out of breath.

"I ran into a stupid meteor shower," he said. "Are the guys from the League of Superheroes here yet?"

"Not yet," I said. "Did you disarm the satellite?"

"Did I have a choice?" he said bitterly. "I

didn't want to get beat up by the League of Superheroes, did I?"

"Well, I guess we'll just have to keep using the same boring old practice dummies at the League," said Tiffany.

"Yeah, what a pity," I said.

"You know," said Nastyboy, "you two jerks sure look familiar. Where do I know you from?"

"Nowhere," I said.

I motioned to Pete Delete. He took out the Power Blacker-Outer. It looked like a flashlight with lots of wires coming out of it. It had a long silver tip.

"No," said Nastyboy, "I know I've seen you before."

"You met us on the satellite dish in space," said Tiffany.

"No, I mean before that," said Nastyboy. He reached out and ripped off my mask.

"Hey!" I shouted.

"I thought so!" he yelled. "You're that little wimp from school, Max Silver!" He turned to Tiffany. "And you — you must be his stupid teenage sister, Tiffany. Hey, wait till I tell the kids at school — Maximum Boy is wimpy little Max Silver, and Maximum Girl is his stupid teenage sister, Tiffany!"

Pete Delete was too fascinated by the conversation to zap Nastyboy with the Power Blacker-Outer. I grabbed it out of Pete's hands, jabbed it at Nastyboy and pressed the ON button. There was a little zapping noise, but nothing else happened.

"Hey, what the heck are you doing to me, you little wimp?" said Nastyboy.

He grabbed at my waist, found the waistband of my underpants and yanked it up high. I couldn't believe it — Maximum Boy was getting a wedgie in uniform!

"Fartmeister, you dork!" I shouted.

I punched him in the nose and stomped hard on his foot at the same time.

"Yowch!" he yelled.

"Hey, Max, you need any help?" called Tiffany.

"Not just now, thanks," I called back.

I did the one martial arts move I know and threw Trevor Fartmeister over my shoulder. He flew through the air and landed on a fire hydrant.

"Yowch!" he yelled again.

"Now, Pete," I said, "let me have that Mind-Eraser."

Pete handed me the black box with the

toggle switches and glowing buttons. I walked up to Trevor, who was just getting up off the fire hydrant and zapped him with the Mind-Eraser.

"Hey, Silver," said Trevor, "what the heck do you think you're d — ?" And then he stopped. He frowned. He stared at me in confusion. "Do I know you?" he asked.

"No, you don't," I answered. "And I don't want to meet you, either. Get out of my sight, so I don't have to look at your ugly face a minute longer."

Trevor frowned. He looked down at his Nastyboy uniform. He didn't seem to recognize it.

"Where'd I get these stupid clothes?" he asked.

"I don't know," I said, "but I don't think you need them any longer."

I focused my disintegrator beam on his uniform, and it began to dissolve. His sweatshirt slowly turned to powder. The same thing was happening to his shoes. And his pants. As Tiffany, Pete, and I watched in amazement, all of Trevor Fartmeister's clothes turned to powder.

Trevor's face got very red. He turned and ran away as fast as he could.

"Well," said Tiffany, "I think we've seen the last of Nastyboy."

"I *hope* we've seen the last of him," I said. "We've certainly seen everything else."

Tiffany and I were sitting in the Oval Office, being thanked by the President.

"Well," said the President, "congratulations to you both on defeating the worst bully in the entire universe."

"Thank you, sir," I said. "Although I don't know how long the Power Blacker-Outer will keep Trevor's powers down to those of a normal school bully. Maybe a long time. Maybe not."

"In the meantime," said Tiffany, "millions of people will be able to poop in peace."

The President smiled proudly. "They will never know what a debt they owe you."

ABOUT THE AUTHOR

When he was a kid, author Dan Greenburg used to be a lot like Maximum Boy — he lived with his parents and sister in Chicago, he was skinny, he wore glasses and braces, he was a lousy athlete, he was allergic to milk products, and he became dizzy when exposed to math problems. Unlike Maximum Boy, Dan was never able to lift locomotives or fly.

As an adult, Dan has written more than fifty-five books for both kids and grown-ups, which have been reprinted in twenty-three countries. His kids' books include the series The Zack Files, which is also a TV series. His grown-up books include *How to Be a Jewish Mother* and *How to Make Yourself Miserable*. Dan has written for the movies and TV, the Broadway stage, and most national magazines. He has appeared on network TV as an author and comedian. He is still trying to lift locomotives and fly.

You never know what he'll dig up.

Meet McGrowl—the courageous canine who's bionic to the bone.

When a bizarre vet turns a decidedly average dog into a bionic beastie, the world's furriest, funniest superhero is born!

You Can Find McGrowl Wherever Books Are Sold
www.scholastic.com/kids

■SCHOLASTIC

MCGT403

Take it to the Max! Learn more about Max Silver's exciting and hilarious adventures. Join him online at

www.scholastic.com/titles/maximumboy

as he tries to save the planet before his curfew.

MAXW1102

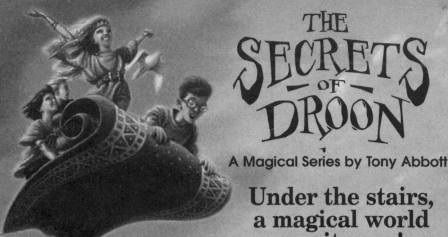

THE SECRETS OF DROON

A Magical Series by Tony Abbott

Under the stairs, a magical world awaits you!

$3.99 each!

- ❏ BDK 0-590-10839-5 — #1: The Hidden Stairs and the Magic Carpet
- ❏ BDK 0-590-10841-7 — #2: Journey to the Volcano Palace
- ❏ BDK 0-590-10840-9 — #3: The Mysterious Island
- ❏ BDK 0-590-10842-5 — #4: City in the Clouds
- ❏ BDK 0-590-10843-3 — #5: The Great Ice Battle
- ❏ BDK 0-590-10844-1 — #6: The Sleeping Giant of Goll
- ❏ BDK 0-439-18297-2 — #7: Into the Land of the Lost
- ❏ BDK 0-439-18298-0 — #8: The Golden Wasp
- ❏ BDK 0-439-20772-X — #9: The Tower of the Elf King
- ❏ BDK 0-439-20784-3 — #10: Quest for the Queen
- ❏ BDK 0-439-20785-1 — #11: The Hawk Bandits of Tarkoom
- ❏ BDK 0-439-20786-X — #12: Under the Serpent Sea
- ❏ BDK 0-439-30606-X — #13: The Mask of Maliban
- ❏ BDK 0-439-30607-8 — #14: Voyage of the *Jaffa Wind*
- ❏ BDK 0-439-30608-6 — #15: The Moon Scroll
- ❏ BDK 0-439-30609-4 — #16: The Knights of Silversnow

Available Wherever You Buy Books or Use This Order Form

www.scholastic.com

▟ SCHOLASTIC

SD1102